John Adams – Space Cadet

and

The Mars Station Incident

Byron F. Abrams

PublishAmerica

Baltimore

First printing

ISBN: 1-59286-400-7
PUBLISHED BY PUBLISHAMERICA BOOK
PUBLISHERS
www.publishamerica.com
Baltimore

Printed in the United States of America

I'd like to dedicate this book to my wife Susan,
for sitting in the living room all those hours by herself,
while I was in the other room, pounding on the keyboard.
I couldn't have done it without you Sue!

I'd like to acknowledge my two grandchildren for their help with this book. To Liz for saying "Way to go Gramps", after reading it, and Tim for his suggestion for the cover.

Also my sister and brother-in-law, Tom and Barb, for their help in proofing the manuscript, and my nephew Mike for his help with my computer.

Also Tim Uphoff of Uphoff Studios, for taking the picture on the back cover. He didn't have much to work with, but did great with what he had! Thanks Tim.

And last but not least, PublishAmerica, for allowing me to get the book published. It's something I've wanted to do for years. Thanks guys and gals!

Chapter One

"Would you look at that? I can't believe my eyes!"

Hank, captain of the pirate ship "Hook," was ecstatic. A freighter, headed for the Mars Station, had just appeared on the view screen.

"Let's get him before he gets any closer to the station."

"We're too close now, Hank. Our chances of getting caught are too great." The pilot squirmed in his seat. "I think we'd better get out of here."

Hank glared at the pilot. "What's the matter, Mike? Scared?"

"No, I'm not scared, Hank. I'm just careful. If there's a defender anywhere close by, we've had it. We'd better pick on a freighter a little farther away from the station."

Grabbing the pilot by the collar, and heaving him out of his seat, Hank sat down. Adjusting the controls for a shot at the freighter, he turned to the pilot.

"You may be chicken, Mike, but I'm not. We'll stop this freighter, board it, get what we want, and be gone, before any defender has a chance to attack us."

"Hank, think about it. We're almost in sight of the station. It has several defenders based there. There could be one on top of us almost instantly."

"Mike, go away. You bother me."

Turning back to the control panel, Hank flipped the switch that armed the ion torpedoes. Then he watched the three target lights flicker yellow, then amber, then red. Pressing the fire switch, he sent an ion torpedo screaming towards the freighter.

The S.S. Monitor shuddered as Hank's shot hit it broadside.

"Damage control to the bridge, NOW!" Captain Marshall yelled into the intercom. Picking himself up off the floor, he called to the helmsman, "Any sign of a defender?"

"Sorry, Sir! No sign of one," the helmsman called back. "The screen is blank. Whoa, wait a second. Here's one now."

Suddenly, appearing on the screen as it dropped out of hyper-drive, the sleek, wicked looking defender blazed past the bow of the freighter, heading in a straight line for the pirate ship. At the same instant, Hank, realizing what was happening, started to turn away, and was gaining speed to try for hyper-drive to escape.

A blazing white light streamed from the front of the defender, as it fired it's opto cannon. The rear cones of the pirate ship disintegrated as the light sliced through them. Separated from the ship, the cones floated slowly away, while the pirate ship came to a halt and hovered in space.

"All right," Captain Marshall exulted. "There's one pirate that's not going to get away."

Turning to the comm he pushed a button. "This is the S.S. Monitor, requesting permission to dock. The ship is damaged and will need to be near a repair pod."

"Roger Monitor," came the reply. "Use docking bay twelve, and we can start repairs immediately. We'll also have a handler-bot there to unload you. Sure glad the cargo is safe. We've been looking forward to receiving it. A meal of real food will be nice once again. Mars Station out."

"Roger, Mars Station. Docking bay twelve. Monitor out."

The S.S. Monitor turned, and slowly approaching Mars Station, nosed into docking bay twelve.

As soon as the air lock cycled, Captain Marshall stepped out into the repair area. Two guards standing there, approached him, and saluted. One of them, shaking his head, spoke.

"We're here to get your story on what happened, Sir."

"It's simple. We were approaching the station to unload and were hit by the pirate's torpedo. They're getting awful brave, hitting us this close to the station. At least it didn't damage us too bad. It could have been worse."

"Yes, sir. The torpedo must have been set for light contact. That way it acted as a battering ram. If it had been set on full power, there wouldn't have been anything left of your ship!"

The other guard spoke up.

"Thanks for your input Captain. We'll get you up and running as quickly as possible. Hopefully, the pirates will be stopped before long. If they get on the station, we won't be able to stop them. They'll own this part of the system then."

Chapter Two

It was a clear, cool, day in March. The sun was shining brightly, as John Adams walked down Academy Way toward the Glenn Space Academy. Smiling to himself, as he thought of the events that had taken place on his way to becoming a space cadet, he failed to hear the warning warble of the emergency vehicle. Lost in thought, he almost didn't realize what was happening. Understanding just in time what was going on, he jumped for the curb, catching the toe of one shoe on it as he did so. As he fell, he managed to twist so he could to use his arms to help break his fall. Landing flat on his stomach, he felt water splashing on him, as the vehicle raced by.

Slowly getting up, and cursing, as he tried to shake the water off, he turned to see the vehicle racing on down the street, spraying water from it's wheels as it sped away. The recent rainstorm had left it's mark on the roadways. Knowing his appointment with Captain Barnes was only a few minutes away, he started on toward the academy. He didn't have a whole lot of time to kill.

Walking into the lobby of the academy a couple of minutes later, he immediately attracted the attention of the receptionist. Looking him up and down, she asked, "Where did you get that uniform Cadet? Buy it from the city dump?"

"All right, all right" John answered rather testily. "I got splashed by an emergency vehicle back down the road, and I didn't have time to change. I'll step into the rest room and clean myself up the best I can".

"Yeah, you'd better do that. Captain Barnes is in a bad mood this morning. He's just received some bad news from the Mars Station. I'm not sure just what it is, but he's pretty shook up over it."

"Just my luck," John muttered as he stepped into the restroom. Grabbing some paper towels he tried to brush his uniform clean, but actually made it worse, as he spread the stains instead of erasing them. Groaning at his misfortune, he threw the towels into the wastebasket, and headed for Captain Barne's office.

Knocking at the captain's office door, and then waiting for the gruff, "Come in," John opened the door, and entered. Saluting smartly, he stood at attention until the captain glanced up, and returned his salute. His eyes widening slightly, as he examined John's uniform, the Captain asked, "What's the matter Cadet? Sleep in your clothes last night?"

"No sir," John replied. "An emergency vehicle and I tangled just down the road, and I came out second best."

"Well, change that uniform just as soon as you can. But we have more important things to discuss right now. I just received word this morning that a pirate raid was attempted right next to the Mars Station. They're getting bolder all the time. They captured the pirates this time, but I'm afraid the station itself is going to come under fire if this continues."

Leaning back in his chair, the captain studied John for a moment. "We're looking for someone willing to go to the station, and update the defense mechanisms. You have the qualifications to do the job. Your scores were tops at the academy. However, there could be some danger involved in doing it."

The captain got up from his chair, and walked around the desk. Seating himself on the edge of it, he studied John for a moment.

"We can't force you to do it," he said. "It's strictly a volunteer mission. However, you're the most qualified student of your class. We need somebody with your knowledge to go to the station, and update the equipment. The station won't be able to withstand a full assault on it unless the defense machinery is improved. You're the best man for the job."

John stood there for a few seconds, contemplating what the captain had just said. Then looking up, he grinned and said, "Yes, Sir. I'll do my best. I'm your man."

"Good! We need your expertise. Dismissed!"

Chapter Three

Bart McNab was furious. Storming into the control center of the small outpost, on an asteroid just outside of Mar's jurisdiction, he slammed his fist onto the desk, as he sat down in front of it.

"Just what did Hank think he was doing, taking on a freighter that close to the station? He knows we aren't ready to take it over yet. Now we've got to move our schedule up, to make up for his mistake. We don't have all of our ships equipped with the new opto cannons yet."

Jan Green cringed at the communications consol. He knew when Bart was mad; it was best to ignore him, if possible.

"Anything coming through?" Bart asked as Jan studied the readouts.

"Nothing new, Bart. It's just the same old static. I don't think there's anything close enough to detect us."

"I don't pay you to think," Bart yelled at him. "You just do your job, and keep your eyes and ears open. If we're found, before we're ready to attack, we're lost." With that Bart stormed out of the control room.

With a sigh of relief, Jan relaxed at the consol. Nothing seemed to be happening. The speakers were emitting nothing but static, and the visual displays were showing nothing but empty space.

Bart walked into the crew quarters and caught two of his men playing cards. "O.K., you two. Get your rear ends up, and out on the repair dock. We've got weapons to install on the ships. We don't have time for your tomfoolery. Move it!"

The two men got up, and left the room, avoiding Bart's eyes as they did so.

"Bunch of no-gooders." Bart mumbled to himself. "Wish we had some dedicated men around here. Maybe our job would be easier. I'll get Hank for this."

Walking out on the observation deck, Bart watched the men scurrying around the small ships. The installation of the opto cannons was proceeding at a slower pace than he'd like. Because of Hank's ship being confiscated by the Mars Authority, his timetable had to be stepped up. He wasn't sure they could be done before they were found out.Turning and walking back into the crew's quarters he muttered, "Yep, Hank's gonna get his."

Bart strode on down to the workshop. Two men had an opto-cannon on the bench, spot-welding the brackets that held the cannon on the ship. As Bart watched, the men rolled the cannon over, and began to weld brackets onto the bottom of it.

Walking up to the bench, he watched as one man held the cannon, and the other ran a bead of weld down the side of the bracket. Examining it critically, he could find nothing wrong with the job.

"Good job guys. I wish everyone here were as conscientious as you two. We'd be a lot further along if they were."

As he turned and walked on out to the landing pad, Brad Pierce turned and looked at Bob Norton.

"Can you believe that?" he asked. "Old Bart actually saying we're doing a good job? He must be slipping."

"Yup, he must be losing it." Ken replied. "Wonder what he'd say, if he knew we were using inferior welding rods? Bet he wouldn't be so quick to compliment us then!"

Chapter Four

John awoke the next morning to find a message on his tele-viewer. The red led was blinking rapidly, signifying a Space Command message.Pushing the covers back, and swinging his legs to the floor, he pressed the receive button. A second later, the screen turned blood red, and a skull and crossbones appeared. Then the words "If you go to Mars, you die!" scrolled onto the screen.

John sat there, looking at the screen in astonishment. This was the Space Command's private frequency. No one outside the Space Command had the proper equipment to use it. Then, suddenly, it dawned on him. This had come from Space Command! Someone besides Captain Barnes knew of his orders. There was a pirate in Space Command! Getting up, he made a copy of the screen.

Then, going to the closet and picking a clean uniform, he hurried through his morning shower rituals, got dressed, and skipping breakfast, headed for the Space Academy.

Entering the foyer, he walked up to the receptionist, and asked, "Is Captain Barnes in?"

The receptionist looked up from her typing, smiled, and said, "My, you look much better today cadet. Got your uniform cleaned, huh?"

John looked at her sourly. "I happen to have more than one uniform. Now please see if the Captain's in. I don't have all day."

Smiling, she pressed the intercom button, and with a little giggle said, "There's a cadet here to see you sir. I believe it's the same one that got run over by an emergency vehicle yesterday."

John snapped, "I didn't get run over by the vehicle. I was just…"

Captain Barnes' voice came over the intercom. "Send him in."

John strode over to the captain's door, and knocked. When ordered, he opened the door, walked in, and stood at attention, while saluting the captain. The captain returned the salute.

"Come over and sit down cadet. You're out early this morning. What can I do for you?"

John walked over to the desk and sat down. Placing the copy of the screen on the desk he said, "I received this on my tele-viewer this morning. It came through on the Space Command frequency. I'm not quite sure what to do about it."

Captain Barnes turned the paper around, studied it for a moment, and then looked up at John. "Are you sure this came through on our frequency? No one is supposed to have access to it but Space Command."

"I know." answered John. "But it was on our frequency. I couldn't believe my eyes when I saw it. At first, I thought I might be mistaken, but it was definitely our frequency. Either someone on the outside has access to it, or we have a pirate in our midst."

"Hmm." The captain studied the paper for a moment. "O.K. cadet. I'll take this copy for the time being. I've got to do some checking on this. However, your orders still stand. You'll lift off first thing tomorrow morning. Be there!"

The following morning, John arrived early at the Kennedy Space Center. After going through customs and checking his luggage, he decided to have a light breakfast before lifting off.

Going to a small café near the public access area, he sat down at the counter and ordered coffee, two eggs, bacon, and toast. As he waited for his order to arrive, he scanned the other patrons of the café. Seeing nobody he knew, he turned his attention to the cup of coffee the waitress had just brought to him.

"Well, well, look who's here."

The voice came from behind him. As he started to turn to his left, someone sat down on his right. As he hesitated, the voice came again.

"It must be the cadet that got his uniform from the city dump."

John spun to his right; ready to voice a few words of his own, then just sat, and stared. Sitting next to him, dressed to travel, was the receptionist from the space center.

Holding out her hand she said, "Hello, my name's Katy Walls. What's yours?"

After a few seconds John shook hands with her. "My name's John Adams. Are you going to the moon also?"

"Oh yeah, I'm going to the moon also. And from there I'm going on to Mars. You had better get used to me buddy. I'm your backup."

"My backup?" John was incredulous. "You mean they're sending a woman to be my backup? I didn't even know I was getting a backup, but a woman? What's the space command coming to anyway? A woman!"

Katy just smiled. "I think when this is all over, you'll be glad I came along."

Turning back to his breakfast, which the waitress had just brought, John muttered to himself, "A woman. What's the world coming to anyway?"

Finishing his breakfast, John turned to Katy and said, "O.K. backup, we've got an hour to kill before lift off. What'll we do?"

Spinning around on her stool she snapped, "My name's Katy, cadet, and don't you forget it!"

Flustered, and red faced, John said, "Sorry Katy. I'll remember it. I didn't mean any harm."

Katy relaxed, and smiled. "That's O.K. John. I just wanted you to know to call me Katy and nothing else. You'll know why soon enough."

Chapter Five

"I'm not talking," Henry 'Hank' Anderson told the Security Force officer. "If I say anything Bart will kill me."

"Look," the officer shot back. "All we want to know is where the pirate base is. You're in enough trouble now to put you away for quite a while. If you come clean and tell us where the base is, it'll go a lot easier on you. We'll find it, one way or another, but it'd be a lot easier on both of us if you talked."

"I ain't saying nothun." Hank snarled. "Go ahead and send me to the caves. The penal colony will be better than being locked up here. If I'm in the caves, at least Bart won't be able to get to me."

"Get him out of here."

The officer thought for a second.

"Just put him in the holding cell for now. We'll want to talk to him again. Maybe, if Bart shows up to get him, we can get Bart."

"No," Hank screamed. "Send me to the caves. If I'm locked up here I'm a dead man. Bart's got eyes and ears here. When he finds out I'm here…"

Suddenly, realizing what he had just said, Hank lowered his head to his hands.

"Oh no," he groaned, "Just shoot me, now."

The security officer sat looking at Hank in shocked silence. Then, reaching across the table, he grabbed Hank by the hair, and jerked his head up.

"You mean to tell me Bart's got operatives here on the station?" Shaking Hank's head violently, the officer yelled, "Is that what you're saying? Answer me!"

"I ain't saying nothun," Hank whispered.

"Lock him up. I want a twenty-four hour guard on him. If any unauthorized person comes within five feet of him, grab them and bring them to me. I'm going to get to the bottom of this."

Hank was trembling as he left the room with the guard right behind him. Starting to turn as he walked ahead of the guard, he was pushed roughly forward.

"Keep moving," the guard ordered.

"I'm going. I'm going. I just don't know why I can't be sent on to the caves. I'd be a lot safer there."

"You mean to tell me you're worried about being safe. After what you've done to those freighters? You've got to be kidding."

"I'm not kidding. I don't want to be here in plain sight where everyone can see me."

"Sorry 'bout that bud. Like it or not, you're bait."

Arriving at the holding cell, the guard opened the door, and standing back, motioned Hank to enter. As the door slammed shut, Hank spun around. Grabbing the bars of the cell door, he pleaded, "Don't leave me like this. I'm a target now for every one of Bart's men. They'll do their best to get rid of me."

"Sorry pal. If you're silly enough to work for the man, you'll just have to take the consequences." With that, the guard spun on his heel and left.

Hank turned and walked over to the bench and sat down. *I'm in big trouble now,* he thought as he lowered his head to his hands. *Why couldn't I've done what Mike said and moved farther away from the station? I wouldn't be in this mess now if I'd just listened to him.*

Raising his head, and staring morosely out through the front of the cell, he saw Mike and the other two crew members walking by, handcuffed, and accompanied by two guards.

As they walked by, Mike turned and caught sight of Hank sitting in the cell. He tried to turn towards the cell, but one of the guards grabbed him.

"Keep moving" the guard shouted.

"Okay, okay." Mike said.

But I'd sure like to get my hands on Hank, he thought. If he had only listened to me, we wouldn't be here now. We would be out there hitting more freighters, and raking in the loot. I hope they throw the book at him. He deserves it.

Chapter Six

John and Katy boarded the moon shuttle just a few minutes before liftoff. Strapping themselves into their assigned seats, they settled down to wait for the shuttle to take off. John laid his head back on the headrest, to try and relax a little. Katy sat up straight, and surveyed the other passengers. Noting nothing out of the ordinary, she settled back in her seat.

Soon a faint rumble began to be heard. The shuttle started to vibrate as the engines were brought up to full power. With a thrust powerful enough to snap their heads back, the shuttle blasted off.

When they had left earth's gravity, the green "Shuttle Airborne" light came on. John remained seated as Katy loosened her seat belt. Standing, she stepped across John's legs to the aisle. As she knelt down in the aisle to snap a loose bootstrap, she happened to glance under John's seat. There, fastened to the bottom of the seat, was a small box, with a red blinking light.

Bomb!

Grabbing John by the shoulder, she said softly, "Don't panic the other passengers, but there's a bomb under your seat. Unfasten you seat belt and stand up slowly. It looks like a small saber bomb. If it is, and does go off, it won't hurt the other passengers."

John straightened up, and started to say, "Don't panic? My gosh Katy…"

Katy slapped her hand over his mouth. "I said be quiet. Unfasten your seat belt and stand up slowly. Do it now!"

John undid the belt, and standing up, moved away as Katy knelt down in the aisle. Putting her hand under the seat, she gently tugged on the box till it dropped off in her hand. John stared at her in astonishment. The other passengers were starting to become agitated, seeing what was going on.

Katy stood up with the box in her hand. Holding her hand in the air she spoke. "It's all right now everybody. Don't be alarmed. Everything's okay.

"Everything's okay? Are you crazy, Katy? Somebody is trying to kill me, and everything's okay? You must be nuts." John was trembling, as he thought of what might have happened.

"Calm down, John. It's under control. You'll be fine. It's only a saber bomb. Just made to kill one person."

Katy reached under the box and pulled out one of the wires hanging there. The red light went out.

John almost fell back into his seat. "Only a saber bomb. Katy, you're nuts."

Shaking his head, John slowly calmed down. "Well, I guess the message I got is going to come true."

The rest of the flight was uneventful. As the shuttle nosed into the landing dock of Moon Base, the pilot's voice came over the speakers.

"Okay, folks. We've arrived at Moon Base. Please wait for the green light to unbuckle your seatbelts. As soon as the klaxon sounds, you'll be able to leave the ship. Hope you've enjoyed the trip."

As the green light came on, the passengers started getting up and grabbing their carry-on luggage. When the klaxon sounded, the outer door swished open, and they started filing out of the ship.

Katy stood up and started to step over John to the aisle.

"Katy, sit down." John said. "I need to talk to you."

"Hey, we're supposed to leave the ship. They'll be returning to Earth shortly."

"I said, sit down!" John snapped. "This is important. They'll check for passengers left behind before disembarking."

Katy gave John a funny look, but sat back down in her seat.

"Okay. I want to know what's going on. Who are you really? Why are you tagging along with me?"

"My name's Katy. I'm your backup. I…"

"I know all that, Katy. But I've received threatening messages, had a bomb planted under my seat, and I don't know what else is going to happen. I've got a right to know what's going on."

Katy thought for a moment.

"All right, John. You're right. You'll find out sooner or later any way. My name really is Katy Walls. I'm a member of an elite ranger group. The Space command keeps us pretty hush-hush. The receptionist role is just a cover. We're trained in the latest weapons. That saber bomb is one of the latest weapons to be certified. If that bomb had gone off, it would have shot a three foot laser beam right straight up, frying you instantly, without hurting anyone else. The job you are going to do is important enough for me to 'tag along,' as you put it. Oh, and by the way, I'm your backup!"

John, stunned, sat there looking at Katy. Finally, shaking his head, he said, "I don't know what to think. But I'll say one thing, Katy. You can be my backup any time!"

Katy smiled. "Thanks for that, John. Now, shall we get off this tub? We've got work to do. If you don't get those generators working, this whole section of space will belong to the pirates."

"I understand that Katy. I'll do my best. Well, let's get off this 'tub' as you call it, and see what happens next. Who knows, maybe things will quiet down now."

"Let's hope so." Katy said. "We'll soon find out."

Chapter Seven

Jan Green was sitting at the communications consol, twiddling dials, when Bart walked into the room. "There's nothing coming through Bart. Still pretty quiet."

"Good. Get me Butch on channel twelve. We've got to do something about Hank. He's liable to blow the whole operation, if we don't stop him. I need to find out where they're keeping him. If they send him to the caves it'll be harder to get to him."

"Will do. I'll let you know just as soon as he contacts us." Jan twirled the frequency dial to the channel twelve range, then pressed the button underneath the dial. "O.K., the signal's on its way. Butch will reply just as soon as he can, without being caught."

As Bart turned to leave the room, he said, "Let me know just as soon as you hear from him. I'm afraid Hank is going to meet with a little accident."

When he was out of earshot Jan said aloud, "Boy, I'd hate to be in Hank's shoes."

A few minutes later, a red light lit up on Jan's consol, as a small buzzer sounded. Jan spoke into the intercom, "Butch is on Bart."

Bart hurried into the communications room, and picking up the mike, spoke into it. "Butch, I'll make this short and sweet.

Hank's got to go. See to it."

Laying the mike back down on the consol, he turned and walked out without another word.

Jan sat there listening to the static coming from the speakers. He spoke aloud again, "Yes sir, I would sure hate to be in Hank's shoes."

Butch replaced the radio in it's holder, and walking to the door, opened it slowly. The small room he was in was toward the rear of the station, and hadn't been used for several years. It made a perfect place for him to contact the pirate base without getting caught. Seeing no one close enough to the room to see him leave, he slipped out of the room and closed the door. Then he nonchalantly headed to his quarters.

Entering, he walked over to his desk, unlocked the top drawer, and withdrew a small vial of yellow liquid. Smiling as he slipped it into his pocket, he thought, *This'll take care of Hank.*

Locking the door behind him as he left his quarters, he headed for the kitchen.

Chapter Eight

John and Katy exited the shuttle and entered the moon base. There was a group of people at the back of the entryway, waiting to be cleared to enter the dome proper. Katy watched them as she and John approached with their luggage. Nothing seemed to be out of the ordinary, as the people were being admitted one by one to the interior of the dome. Soon the two of them were inside the dome itself. Just inside the entryway were several small shops selling food, souvenirs, books and newspapers, and various other items. It was a noisy place, with people talking loudly, several tele-viewers giving news broadcasts, and loud speakers announcing arrivals and departures.

Suddenly John heard his name announced over the speakers. "Cadet Adams, please report to Space Command Office B. Cadet Adams, please report to Space Command Office B."

John looked at Katy and grinned. "Sure don't give us much time to look around do they? I was hoping to be able to wander around just a little bit. Oh well, I guess duty calls."

They headed towards the rear of the public access area. Soon they came to the Space Command Complex. An armed guard turned as they approached, and asked for their ID's. After checking them against a list on his clipboard, he turned and pressed a button. The door slid open to allow them access to the command headquarters. The door slid shut behind them as they entered.In front of them was a long hall with doors lining both sides. Starting down the hall John knocked on the door of office B.

"Come in, if your nose is clean."

John looked at Katy, laughed, and shook his head. Then, opening the door, they stepped into office B.

A small, bearded man, sat behind a desk piled high with books and papers.

"Hello, I'm Professor Heidrich."

Getting up from his chair, the professor walked around the desk, and shook hands with John and Katy.

"I hope you two don't mind being sent right on to Mars. We need to get you started on your mission as soon as possible. Time's a wasting. The sooner you can get started on the alterations, the sooner we can make the Mars Station safe. I've got the blueprints of the station here, so you can examine them while on your way.They should be able to help you decide what to do to upgrade the defense system."

"Thanks, Professor. I'm sure they'll come in handy. I've got a pretty good idea of how everything is set up, but the blueprints will help fill in the pieces. By the way, I'm surprised to see a non-military person in command headquarters."

The professor chuckled. "I'll tell you what John. You're going to have a lot of surprises before your career in the Space Command is over. Just keep your wits about you, and everything will turn out all right."

The professor turned and picked up a roll of paper and handed it to John.

"Here are the blueprints. The Mars Ship is due for take off in thirty minutes. Better get aboard and settled down. If you've never been on a Space Command fighter, it'll be quite an experience."

"Thanks Professor. I'll look these over while I'm on the defender. Yes, I understand those ships are something else. It'll be an interesting ride I'm sure. Ready to go Katy?"

"Sure thing. Let's get the show on the road."

The professor shook hands with them, and then said, "Good luck, you two. You'll need it."

Chapter Nine

Hank sat in the back corner of his cell, watching the people come and go, hoping against hope he wouldn't see anybody else he knew. The minutes spread into hours as he sat there watching. Gradually he started to relax, as nothing out of the ordinary happened.

About mealtime, the guard brought his meal to him on a tin plate. Sliding the plate through the access slot, it rested on the attached shelf. As Hank got up to get the plate, he caught a glimpse of someone he thought he knew. Hurrying to the front of the cell, he tried to see through the crowd of people, but couldn't find the person again.

Picking up the plate, he turned to go back to his seat. As he sat down, and pulled the cover off the food, he got to thinking. What if the food was poisoned? What if the person he had caught a glimpse of had brought the food to the guard? What if he ate the food? Would it poison him or was he just imagining things?

"GUARD, GUARD," Hank yelled.

When the guard approached Hank said, "This food has been poisoned. They're trying to kill me."

"Oh, sure," the guard said. "And I'm a yellow monkey."

"No, I'm serious. Bart knows I'm here. He'll do his best to

kill me. He'll be afraid I'll talk. I tell you it's poisoned. Take it back and test it if you don't believe me. I won't eat it. It's poisoned, I tell you."

The guard shrugged his shoulders. "Just let it set there and rot. I'm not taking it back."

As he turned to walk away, the officer that had questioned Hank stepped in.

"I just happened to be walking by, and heard you two talking. He could be right. If Bart does have operatives on the station, he'd leave orders to get him. I'll take it down to the lab myself and have it checked. If there is something wrong with it, we'll know for sure Bart's people are on the base."

Hank got up and slid the tray through the slot. The officer took it and walked away.

"I'm not bringing you anything else," the guard growled. "You can just starve, as far as I'm concerned."

"Don't worry." Hank replied. "I'd rather die from starvation than from poisoning."

An hour later the guard came, and unlocked the cell door. "Come with me," he commanded.

Hank got up, and approached the front of the cell. "Where are we going?" he asked.

"You're wanted in the interrogation room," was all the guard would say.

As they entered the room, Hank saw the security officer, and the station commander, sitting at the table.

"Sit down," the officer commanded. After he had done so, the officer continued. "You were right about the food. There was enough poison in it to kill a horse."

"I knew it, I knew it." Hank yelled. "You've got to protect me. Bart'll have me killed. He's out to get me. I'm a dead man unless you do something."

"Now don't panic," the officer said. "Would you know any of Bart's people if you saw them? If we brought you the station's photo list, could you identify any of them, if you saw the pictures?"

"I could try. I'm sure I don't know everybody Bart has working for him, but I do know several of them."

"Take him back to his cell. Keep a close watch on him. We need him now."

"Let's go." Grabbing Hank by his shoulder, the guard led him out of the room.

Walking him back to his cell, the guard spoke. "If you know what's good for you, you'll identify every one of Bart's men you see in the list. You can't be in any more trouble than you are right now."

Hank looked at the guard but said nothing.

"Believe me," the guard added. "You've got nothing to loose by doing so."

Chapter Ten

As John and Katy left the Space Command Complex and started across the public access area, he turned toward her.

"I think I'll step in here and pick up a magazine. It'll give me something to do when I get tired of reading blueprints."

Just as he turned to enter the shop, he heard a sharp 'ZZZZZTT' sound.

"DOWN!" Katy yelled, and shoved him roughly onto his knees. At the same time, a wicked looking ray gun mysteriously appeared in Katy's hand.

"Stay down," Katy ordered, as she slowly turned to survey the crowded concourse. Seeing nothing out of the ordinary, she decided the shooter had fled.

The shot had missed John by mere inches, but it hadn't missed the wooden Indian standing by the door of the small tobacco shop. It had a hole drilled neatly into it's forehead.

John got slowly to his feet. He turned and stared at Katy. The ray gun had disappeared.

"I didn't know you were armed. You're full of surprises."

"We women have to take care of ourselves." Katy smiled. "I'm sure glad nobody was hurt. We could've had quite a problem. I was told that Bart wanted you out of the picture real bad. I can see that I'm going to have to be more careful from now on."

"I know what you mean." John replied. "I'm going to have to wake up also. I was told it would be dangerous, but never expected anything like this. I figured most of my trouble would be on Mars. Let's get on that ship before anything else happens."

Approaching the Space Command Defender, John stopped and stared. He had seen pictures of them, but had never seen one in real life. It bristled with weapons. Opto cannon front and rear. Smaller barrels on the top and sides meant high-intensity ray guns. John knew it also had sonic bombs and ion torpedoes.

It was much smaller than John had thought. Having only a crew of three, and not staying in space for any length of time, the defender didn't need to be large. After looking at it for a moment, he turned to Katy.

"This ship is nothing but a weapon with rockets. I'd hate to have this thing chase me down a dark alley."

"I know what you mean," Katy replied. "The defender is a war machine. If we ever find out where Bart's hideout is, just one of these ships will make short work of it. Well, we'd better get ourselves aboard. The Space Command doesn't like to be kept waiting. We've got a job to do."

Approaching the runway to the ship, they were stopped by two very efficient looking guards.

"ID's please."

After thoroughly checking their ID'S, one of the guards picked up a small retina checker. Placing it first over John's eyes, and then Katy's, he checked to be sure their retinas matched the one's in their records. After doing this, he asked, "Any weapons?"

"Two," Katy answered.

"One permitted."

With that, she handed the ray gun to the guard.

"You'll get this back just as soon as you arrive at the station. Go ahead and board."

Walking up the runway, and into the ship, they were met by a ship's officer.

"This way please."

Following him, they were led to a section in the middle of the ship. Entering a small cubicle, they sat down in a hammock like device, and were strapped in.

"Not the fanciest accommodations in the world," the officer said. "But this is not a passenger cruiser either. The ride won't be too long. We are going into hyper-drive a lot sooner than normal. We have orders to get you there as soon as possible. Just relax." With that, he turned and left the cubicle, shutting the door behind him.

John turned his head and looked at Katy. She was lying there with her eyes closed.

"Aren't you just a little bit nervous?" he asked. "This is my first time in one of these. I thought you'd be shaking in your shoes."

Katy rolled her head towards him and opened her eyes.

"John," she said, "Just relax. There's nothing to it. This is my seventh trip to Mars Station. Now be quiet. I want to take a nap." Smiling, she closed her eyes.

John just shook his head. "Guess I've got a lot to learn," he muttered.

Lying there, John got to thinking. *What if I can't do this? What if I don't get the generators fixed in time? What if the pirates fire on the station before I get the shields back up to full power?*

Katy turned her head and glanced at John. He was lying there with a worried look on his face.

Grinning, she said, "Think maybe they should have chosen someone else for the job?"

John looked at Katy. "What did you say?"

Katy smiled. "I just asked if maybe they should have chosen someone else for the job. I could tell by the look on your face you're worried. Relax John. You'll do fine."

"I sure hope so, Katy, but it makes me wonder."

"I'm sure it does. But you'll have all the help you need to get the generators fixed. You'll do fine."

Chapter Eleven

Bart McNab was restless. He paced the floor of the communications room. *Why doesn't Butch check in?* he thought, as he walked. *What's his problem? He should have checked in by now. A simple task like that shouldn't be any problem. He's had plenty of time.*

Even as he was thinking this, the signal arrived. The red light came on, and the buzzer sounded. Jan Green punched in the code that brought Butch's face to the screen. It wasn't a pleasant face. Butch was scowling as he stared into the screen.

"All right, already." Bart snapped. "What's the problem? I gave you a simple task. Don't tell me you can't pull it off. All you had to do was slip a little poison into Hank's food. How hard can that be?"

"Look Bart. I did poison Hank's food. I put enough poison in it to kill three people. Somehow or another he figured out what was going on. He wouldn't touch his food. He threw such a fit; one of the guards must've had the food checked. It wasn't long after the food was served, that the guard took him to the interrogation room. He must've spilled his guts. They brought him back to his cell under double guard. We can't get within twenty feet of him now."

Bart slammed his fist down on the consol. "We've got to

stop him! If he rats on our people on the station we're done for. Get your people together, and figure out a way to stop him. If he's not done away with, we're dead. Do it, and do it now!"

Bart turned and stormed out of the room. Butch shook his head and said, "Well, he's in his regular good mood isn't he? I'll get everyone over here together, but don't know what we can do. They're going to keep a tight lid on him now."

Jan shook his head. "It doesn't look too good, does it? I'm beginning to wonder if things aren't going to go downhill fast. I'll keep the frequency open in case you need to contact Bart. Good luck. You're going to need it."

Butch's face disappeared from the screen.

Jan shook his head again. "It doesn't look good at all."

Hank was nervous. He had spent almost two hours looking at photographs of the station's occupants, but hadn't recognized a single one. He flipped another page. Still no one he knew.

"Well," the officer asked. "I thought you said you knew some of Bart's men. What are you doing? Trying to cop out on me?"

"Hey, I told you I didn't know everybody Bart has on the station. If I see one, I'll let you know."

As he spoke, he flipped another page. There! Right in the center of the page! A picture of Butch.

"All right, here's a picture of Butch. He's one of Bart's main men. And he's working here on the station. I told you I'd know one if I saw one." Hank spun the book around so the officer could see it.

"Which one is he?"

"There, the one in the middle of the page"

"You mean this one?" the officer asked pointing at Butch's picture.

"Yep, that's Butch. I don't know his real name, but he's Bart's second in command."

Hank looked at the officer.

"I told you Bart has people on the station. If his plans work out, he's going to take over the station, and use it as his base of operations. He'll control all of this part of space, and be able to loot freighters at will."

The officer looked at the picture again, his face becoming grim as he did so. He looked up at the guard standing behind Hank.

"Go get some help, then go round up Lt. Haskell, and bring him to me. I want to see him now."

The guard turned and left the room. Hank sat there nervously for a moment then spoke. "I want to go back to my cell. If Butch sees me here, he'll know I ratted on him. I'll be a dead man."

"You just stay right here. Haskell will be under guard. He won't be able to touch you."

"Not now, maybe. Later, though, he'll tell Bart. Bart will make sure I get mine." Hank started sweating. "I'm the same as a dead man now. I want you to send me to the caves."

The officer laughed. "I'll bet you that Bart has people in the caves too. I doubt we could send you anywhere that Bart doesn't have people. We've got to stop him now. If we don't, he's going to be so big, we won't be able to stop him, without using most of our forces to do it. There will be lots of deaths if we don't stop him now."

The door to the room opened and Hank spun around. The guard hurried into the room.

"The Lieutenant has left the station. He stole a runabout and left about ten minutes ago. Command central doesn't know where he went. He just disappeared!"

Chapter Twelve

As John lay in his hammock, the fighter began to shudder. Suddenly, a voice came from a small speaker in a corner of the cubicle.

"I just wanted you two to know we're about to lift off. There will be a sharp thrust for a few seconds till we're away from the moon. Then when we go into hyper-drive, you'll have a queasy feeling for several seconds, as your bodies try to adjust to the difference in the time frame. You'll soon recover from the effects. We'll let you know in plenty of time before we jump. Just relax and you'll be fine."

Just as the voice disappeared, John felt the pressure begin to build up. As he lay there, it built up more and more. John felt like an elephant had stepped down, right in the middle of his stomach. Just as he began to wonder if he was going to make it, the pressure let up. He looked over at Katy. She turned her face towards him, and smiled.

"You'll get used to it," she said. Then she lay her head back down on the headrest, and shut her eyes.

How in the world can anybody get used to this? John thought as he settled back in the netting.

Picking up his magazine, John opened it, and tried to read. But after a few moments he laid it aside and just rested. *Oh well. Maybe some day I will get used to this, but I doubt it.*

"Okay, you two. Hyper-drive coming up on the count of five. Get ready. One... Two... Three... Four... Five!"

John groaned. He felt like his stomach had dropped down to his feet. No, that couldn't be right. His feet were twisted around his head. No wait, his head was between his knees. No wait; his knees were wound around his neck. He felt like his whole body was twisted up and falling to pieces. He wanted to look at Katy, but couldn't turn his head. He wondered if she looked like a pretzel too.

Just as quick as they started, the feelings left him. Everything popped back into place.

"Wow! I didn't know I could be so torn to pieces. I'm glad I don't have to go through that every day. I don't believe I could stand it."

Katy laughed. "I know what you mean. As many times as I have gone through it, I'm still bothered by it. It's hard to believe your body isn't harmed in any way. The feeling is all in your mind."

John asked, "Is it the same when we drop out of hyper-drive?"

"Yep. You'll feel just the same. It only lasts for a few seconds, but it seems like hours. Some of the rocket jockeys say it doesn't bother them, but don't believe it. It affects everybody the same way."

"Well I'm just glad it's over with for now. I think I'll relax for a few minutes." John scooted around to a more restful position. "If you can relax in this bucket, that is."

John awoke suddenly.

"Gee, I must have dozed off." Hearing no response he looked over at Katy. Katy wasn't there. John glanced around the cubicle. No sign of her. Unbuckling his straps, John sat up. *I wonder if the artificial gravity unit is on,* he thought. Standing up, his feet stayed on the floor. *Yep, I guess it is.*

Walking over to the door, John opened it, and stepped through.

The hallway was narrow but short. To the right was the closed door of the bridge. To the left were several doors leading off the hallway. They were all closed. John turned to the left. He knew he wouldn't be allowed on the bridge except in an emergency.

As he started down the hall, he heard voices coming from behind one of the doors. He stopped and listened. Then proceeding slowly down the hall he stopped at the second door. The voices were coming from there.

"Look, I told you I know nothing about it. I'm only going to Mars for a little rest and recreation."

"Yeah, sure lady. We know better than that. You and that cadet are up to something, and I'm going to find out what it is."

A sharp smack, followed by a curse, came through the door. "I don't have all day, so you had better talk if you don't want more of that."

They've got Katy! John thought, as he started looking around for a weapon. Spying a fire extinguisher hanging on the wall, John grabbed it. Walking up to the door, John slowly started to turn the doorknob. The door was locked!

John suddenly reached out, and knocked loudly. Silence. Then a man's voice, "Who is it?"

"It's Haskell. We need to talk."

"Haskell? I was told you escaped, and went back to the outpost. What are you doing here?"

"That's what Bart wants everybody to think. I used false papers to get aboard. I need to see you now."

With a sharp click the door opened. The man behind the

door suddenly realized it was a trick. But he was too late. With a loud 'whoosh,' John released the foam from the extinguisher, right into the man's face. With a scream, the man backed up, trying to rub the foam out of his eyes. John stepped in, and with a quick swing, smashed the extinguisher into the man's head. He went down in a heap.

"Way to go cadet."

John spun around. Katy was strapped to a chair. He hurried over to undo the straps.

"How in the world did you ever get into this? I thought you were my backup. Are you O.K.?"

"I'm fine. He came in while I was asleep, and drugged me. It's hard to believe Bart could get a man on a ship like this. Thanks for getting me out of this. I thought I was going to be in for a rough time. By the way, how did you know about Lt. Haskell?"

John laughed. "As we were leaving the moon base, I heard two of the guards talking. They mentioned he was missing and was wanted for questioning. I took a chance when using his name, but didn't know what else to do."

"You did fine. Now let's find some help and get this jerk confined, so he won't be any more trouble. And John, thank you!"

John opened the door, and stepped out into the hall. Looking both ways, and not seeing anybody, he decided to go forward to the bridge. As he approached the bridge door, it opened and the Captain stepped out. "I'm sorry, son, but no one is allowed on the bridge but the crew."

"I know, Sir." John answered. "But I need some help. We just cornered one of Bart's men in a room back down the hall, and need some help in getting him in a safe place."

"One of Bart's men on this ship? Come on son, you don't

expect me to believe that do you? One of his men couldn't get within a hundred feet of this ship. And you expect me to believe that one is on the inside of it. I don't think so!"

"Look Sir, I'm not lying to you. He had Katy strapped to a chair, and was trying to get her to talk. He's probably got a sore head right now, but when he comes to, he could be trouble. We need to find a place to put him where he can't cause any more problems."

The captain turned back to the door. "Larson, front and center."

A man, wearing a lieutenant's uniform, stepped through the door. "What's up Cap? Need a baby sitter?"

"Go with the cadet and find out what's going on. He says he has one of Bart's men cornered. If he does, I'll kiss his foot when we get back to moon base!"

"Cap," the lieutenant grinned. "If he does, I'll be there with my camera." Then looking at John he said, "Let's go see what kind of trouble you've been into."

The two men turned and went back down the hall to the room John had just left. As they entered the room, the Lieutenant stopped so suddenly, John ran into him. John looked over his shoulder, and saw Katy sitting in the chair, with a small disrupter aimed at the man in the corner.

The Lieutenant raised one hand, and said, "Whoa, sister. You're not allowed to have weapons on board. You'd need a ranger rating to carry that here. Better give it to me."

Katy just smiled, then reached into the pocket of her vest, and pulling out a small case, tossed it to the lieutenant.

"Open it." she said. "And don't call me sister. My name's Katy."

The lieutenant flipped the top of the case open, and looking inside, whistled.

"A gold Ranger Badge. Sorry Katy. I didn't know." Shutting the lid, he handed it back. Looking over at the man in the corner he whistled again. "You sure did a job on him Katy. Couldn't have done better myself."

"You've got John to thank for that." Katy said. "Hadn't been for him I would be in a heap of trouble. Instead Bart's man is in a heap on the floor."

The Lieutenant shook his head. "Boy I've sure changed my opinion of you two. Well, we had better get this jerk to a safe place. There's a small freight hold that we can lock him up in. He sure won't be able to get out of there. Wait till the captain hears about this. He's going to be fit to be tied. John, remind me to buy some film as soon as we get back to Moon Base. I'm going to take the best picture of my life."

Chapter Thirteen

Bart had Butch, aka Lt. Haskell, backed into a corner. "Are you sure you weren't followed? The last thing we need is the space command breathing down our necks."

"No, I wasn't followed. I went to hyper-drive as soon as I left the station. I came back to normal space way past the asteroid belt, and then wormed my way back through it to get here. The space command doesn't have a ship that travels slow enough to go through the belt."

"You'd better be right." Bart snapped. "We don't need a confrontation with space command right now. I've got enough problems without them giving me fits. Now, go see if you can get the men to speed up the installation of the cannon. I've lost enough time as it is."

As Butch left the room Bart turned and went to the communications room. "See if you can reach one of the other men on the Mars Station." he told Jan. "We still need a contact there to keep us informed as to what's going on. We don't want any surprises."

"Sure thing Bart. I'll keep trying, and let you know just as soon as I do."

Bart spun on his heel and walked out of the room.

Well, all I can do is keep it on this frequency, and send the reply signal every so often, Jan thought. *Maybe somebody on the station will be smart enough to pick it up.*

Fifteen minutes later, the red light blinked, and the buzzer sounded. Jan thumbed the intercom switch.

"Bart, got a message from the station."

Bart entered at a fast walk. "On the screen."

Jan pressed the screen button, but nothing happened. He pressed it again. Still nothing. The screen remained blank.

Then a voice came from the speaker. "There will be no picture. But hear this. A Space Command Defender left Moon Base a short time ago. It was carrying two extra passengers and went into hyper-drive very soon after blasting off. I'm not sure it is headed for Mars Station, but if it is, they'll be there fairly quickly. Just wanted to let you know."

"Identify yourself," Bart snapped. "Who are you?"

"Sorry, but no way. If I were found out, I couldn't get away the way Butch did." The red light blinked off.

Bart was boiling. "Why can't just one thing go right? I'll find out what's going on if I have to go to Mars Station myself."

Leaving the communications room, Bart walked back to his quarters. Sitting down at his desk, he started thumbing through the manifests listing the goods his men had stolen from the freighters they had stopped. By selling most of the items through his contacts, he had accumulated a fairly large number of credits. But, he was just greedy enough to want more.

Getting up, he began to pace the floor. I can't let us get caught, he thought as he walked. There's too much at stake here. One way or another I've got to get on that station. There's surely some way we can keep the generators from getting fixed before we attack.

Suddenly he spoke aloud. "I'm going to get Butch, and get on that station. There's got to be some way to get that Cadet stopped."

He headed for the door. Going to the storeroom he grabbed his space suit and helmet, then walked out to the airlock. Suiting up, he cycled the air lock and went outside.

The small ships were lined up in a row, with suited figures crawling over most of them. Most of the ships had the telltale sign of the opto-cannon barrel mounted on them. Two ships were having them installed as he watched and two were still waiting their turn.

Four ships to go and he would be ready!

Chapter Fourteen

John was sitting on the edge of his hammock, studying the Mars Station blueprints, when Lt. Larson stepped into the room.

"Well, we're better than halfway there." he said. "Hope you two are okay after your little incident. Bet you never thought something like that would happen on a Space Command Defender!"

Katy looked over at him. "I couldn't believe it, when I came to strapped in that chair. Have you figured out how that guy got on the ship without being seen?"

"No we haven't, Katy. However, you'd better believe we will. When something like this happens, we pull out all the stops, till we understand what happened. This ship was under guard every second it was docked. The two guards that had the midnight shift are being questioned as we speak. One way or another, we'll get to the bottom of it."

Just as the lieutenant turned, and started to leave the room, the captain's voice came from the speaker. "Lt. Larson, have the cadet report to the bridge. We've got a problem here."

"I wonder what's wrong now?" Larson said. Then "OK John, front and center. Let's go see what's bugging the captain. Looks like you're going to get to see the bridge after all."

John jumped up from the hammock, and the two men started

out the door. Katy watched them leave and then mumbled to herself, "Some people have all the luck."

Just then Lt. Larson stuck his head back into the door. "Katy, why don't you come also? If something weird is going on here, we might need a witness. There just might be a panel called over this, and we'll need all the help we can get."

Katy got up, and hurried after the two men, to the bridge. Lt. Larson opened the door, and motioned John and Katy to precede him into the room. The captain spun around in his chair, saw Katy come through the door, and frowned.

"Cap," Lt. Larson spoke. "I asked Katy to come with us. I thought if a panel were called over this, she might be a good witness."

"Good thinking, Lieutenant. You're right. John, come and take a look at this."

John didn't hear him. He was staring at all the knobs, switches, meters, handles, lights, and other controls. Except for the floor and windows, every inch of the walls and ceiling were covered with controls. *Man,* John thought. *This looks like something out of a science fiction movie.*

"Cadet!" The Captain spoke harshly. "I said, come and take a look at this."

"Oops." John said. "Sorry, Sir. I guess I was in a trance. I couldn't believe what I was seeing. What's the problem?"

"Our guidance system seems to be acting up. According to all our motion controls we're in motion. According to our guidance system we're sitting still. We can't make heads or tails out of it."

John walked over to the guidance control panel. He looked at the guidance meter. It showed zero speed. However he could hear the rocket engines humming. If they were sitting still the rockets wouldn't be running. Grasping the handles of the control panel he pulled. It slid out exposing the wires, and other components behind the panel. Bending over, he started inspecting the back of the panel. Everything seemed to be all right. He checked very carefully. Nothing seemed out of place.

He was just about ready to ask to see the motion panel when he saw it. A splice in one of the wires! Following the wire with his finger he traced it up to the back of the meter. This couldn't be right! No wonder the meter wasn't working. Someone had spliced the readout wire to the guidance timer wire. Since the timer had lost it's power it would quit when it's internal battery died. The guidance meter would then reset to zero. With no power it would stay at zero.

"I've found it Sir. Someone's been messing around back here. They've spliced two wires together that don't belong that way. I'll just change them back to the way they belong, and everything should be all right."

John quickly respliced the wires to their original locations. The guidance meter started working again, showing speed and course. "There, that should take care of it." John pushed the panel back into the consol.

"Well done, John. I don't mind telling you, this is one trip I'm glad to have passengers on board!"

John laid the blueprints aside, rubbed his eyes, and turned to look at Katy. She raised her eyes from the book she was reading, and smiled at him.

"I'm sure glad the rest of the trip has been pretty uneventful," she said. "We're just about there now. It won't be long until we drop out of hyper-drive. Mars is just around the corner so to speak. It won't be long till you'll be right in the middle of everything."

"Yeah, I know. I just hope I can get the shields up and running before Bart decides to attack the station. If the shields aren't operating, there won't be too much of a chance of the station coming out in one piece, unless we can get enough ships here to hold Bart's ships off. I understand there's not much chance of that. Most of the Space Command ships are out on the frontier, checking on the outposts there. I guess there's quite a bit of excitement going on out there. I'd sure like to be out there myself, but don't believe there's much chance of that."

"You never know, John. This assignment won't last forever. With your training they won't let you be still for very long. I've got a feeling you'll be going a lot of places, and seeing a lot of things, before you get a chance to rest for very long."

"I hope so, Katy, but guess I had better concentrate on this assignment before starting to worry about something else. I sure hope I can get the shields up and running. That would give the station a better chance of surviving an attack from the pirates."

"Don't worry, John. You'll do fine. Just concentrate on what you have to do, and everything will work out."

The speaker in the corner of the room sounded off. "OK people. Get set. Dropping out of hyper-drive in two minutes."

Shortly, "Okay, on the count of five. One....Two....Three....Four....Five!

John turned into a pretzel again, but in a few seconds it was all over.

"Wow." John shook his head. "Glad that's not an everyday occurrence. I don't think I could take it."

"I know what you mean. Just think, when we leave here to go back to Earth, we'll have to go through with it again. Pleasant thought!"

"Okay, you two." The speaker again. "We'll be landing at the station before long. Make sure you are strapped in, and don't leave anything loose lying around. A flying book could hurt if it hit you in the head."

Katy made sure everything was strapped down, and then lay down on her hammock. Strapping herself in, she lay there quietly until the defender nosed into the dock of the station. Then, unstrapping herself, she followed John out of the room into the hallway. Lt. Larson was standing at the exit with their luggage. "Here you go, guys. Hope you have a good stay on the station. And good luck to you, John. Hope you are successful with your task. It would sure mean a lot to the station."

"Thank you, Sir. Good luck to you too." John shook hands with the lieutenant, and then he and Katy stepped through the door onto the Mars Station platform. At last they had arrived!

They didn't have long to stand on the platform. An armed guard approached them, and asked, "Cadet Adams and Katy Walls?" As they nodded their heads yes, he motioned them to follow him.

"Where are we going?" John asked.

"We're going to the station commander's office." The guard answered. "He wants to see you right away. We're going to need you to start on the shields right away or it may be too late."

"Well I'm ready to start right now." John said. "The sooner the better as far as I'm concerned."

"Good. I'm sure the commander will get you started right away."

As they approached the door to the commander's office, a second guard standing there looked John up and down. "Is this the cadet that's going to save the station? He looks awful young to me. Bet he's still wet behind the ears."

"That's enough, Bud." The first guard spoke. "Give him a chance. You have no idea what he can do. Inform the commander they're here. He wants to see them just as soon as they arrive."

The second guard turned and knocked on the door.

"Yes?" came from inside the room.

"The cadet is here Sir," he said as he opened the door.

"Good, good. Send him in."

As John and Katy started to enter the room, the guard placed his arm in front of Katy. "I'm sorry ma'am, but you'll have to wait outside. They'll be discussing some very important secret data in there."

"Look. I'm John's backup. I have instructions from Captain Barnes not to let him out of my sight. I think that includes the commander's office."

As the guard started to frown, the commander said from inside the room, "It's OK Bud. She has ranger status. We'll not be discussing anything so secret that a ranger can't hear it. Let her come in."

Katy followed John through the door. As she did she turned to Bud and smiled. "No hard feelings I hope?"

"No ma'am." Bud said as he pulled the door shut. He looked over at the first guard and shrugged. "You never know who's who in the space command anymore. Next thing you know we'll be saluting kids."

"There's a lot of kids out there worth saluting, Bud. Well, I've got to get back to my post. Take care."

"See you later."

When the first guard was out of sight, Bud checked in all directions. Seeing nobody watching him, he pulled a small radio from his pocket. Pressing the transmit button he said softly, "They're in the commander's office. Awaiting instructions."

Chapter Fifteen

The red light came on, and the buzzer sounded softly. Jan flicked the switch that changed the frequency to channel twelve. The words "They're in the commander's office. Awaiting instructions," issued from the speaker. Jan hit the intercom button.

"Bart, Bud's on the radio. Wants to know what to do next."

Bart hurried into the room and, removing his helmet, picked up the microphone. "Just hang loose for a little while Bud. Be sure and follow them when they leave. We need to create some kind of diversion so that the cadet won't be able to work on the system. Our ships will be ready to fly in two days. If we can hold them off that long, we may have a chance. Do what you can."

Bart replaced the microphone on it's holder. Turning to Jan he said, "Don't you let anything get by you. We're close enough now that the least little hitch could cause us to lose valuable time. The opto cannons are all installed. All they need is to be charged and tested. Any problem now could be big trouble."

"I'll do my best, Bart." Jan said.

"You're best had better be good enough. Any mistake now, and you'll be accountable." Bart scowled, then spun on his heel and walked out of the office.

Jan shook his head. "Just like Bart," he muttered.

Replacing his helmet, Bart walked down to the docks where the work was going on. Seeing Butch standing with two of the men looking at the blueprints he strode up to them. "How are things going?"

Butch looked up at Bart and smiled. "Everything's going fine here, Bart. We're going to make the deadline no problem. All cannons are installed, and about half of them are charged. As soon as the rest are charged we will take the ships out to the belt and test them. If everything's all right we'll be ready to attack the next day. Right on schedule."

"That's the best news I've heard since we started this job. With any luck at all, in three days we'll be on the station. Then our fortune will be made. The freighters will be ours."

Bart walked over to one of the ships that had been set up to mount an opto cannon. He checked the mounting very carefully, but could see nothing out of place. The cannon was mounted on the front of the ship and could be swiveled forty-five degrees in any direction. A small, but deadly weapon, it looked out of place on the pirate ship.

Turning, he motioned to Butch. As Butch approached, he said, "Let's take this ship out to the asteroid belt and test it. We'll find out whether it really works or not."

"Good idea, Bart. I'll just go get my flight list, and I'll be ready."

Soon, clipboard in hand, Butch returned to the ship. Bart was sitting at the control consol. Butch sat down in the co-pilot's seat and strapped himself in.

"Ready?"

"Ready."

Checking to make sure they were in the clear, Bart lifted the ship off the ground, and headed for the belt. As it came into sight, Bart maneuvered the ship between two huge asteroids. Then he glanced over at Butch, sitting in the co-pilot's seat.

"It's my understanding that these weapons won't cause their targets to explode. They'll just slice through them, cutting them into pieces. We'll find out soon enough. If one of these asteroids explodes when it's hit we're goners."

Butch smiled through his helmet.

"Don't worry, Bart. These are regulation issue weapons. They'll work just like they're supposed to. Let'em have it!"

Bart swiveled the cannon towards the smaller of the two asteroids, and flipped the arm switch. A slight hum sounded for a few seconds, and then the green ready light glowed. Pressing the fire button, a blinding white light streamed from the barrel of the cannon, and neatly sliced off a small section of the asteroid. As it slowly floated away, Bart moved the cannon a few degrees left, and pressed the fire button again. Another small section of the asteroid was sliced off. As it slowly floated away, Bart let out a whoop.

"Well, buddy, I can see it now. Another day, and the Mars Station will be ours. Then we'll control the freight lanes all the way to the outer belts. It'll be easy pickings from now on."

"Let's hope so Bart. If the guys can finish the work in time I think we've got it made."

Smiling, Bart turned the ship around and headed for the base.

Chapter Sixteen

The station commander was speaking. "Now that you know the situation here, you know why we need the station defenses brought up to date. Bart getting the station to use as a base of operations is bad enough. Bart getting the station for what's happening here, that he doesn't know about, would be ten times worse. If he got his hands on the new interstellar ship we're building here, he could become almost invincible. He could pretty much rule this part of space."

The commander shook his head. "If he gets control of that ship, we couldn't touch him."

"I'll sure do my best." John said. "I believe, with a little help, we can have the shields up and running in two or three days."

"You can have who or what you need as soon as you need it. If need be, we'll put every man on the base at your disposal. We need those shields operating as soon as possible."

"Fine. Katy and I will go check the generators now. Just as soon as I figure out what we need, I'll let you know." John stood up. "Again commander, I'll do my best"

"That's good enough for me. You have one of our short-range in-house radios. Any time you press the transmit button you'll be communicating directly with me. I'll see that you get what you need, as quickly as possible. Good luck, Cadet!"

"Thank you, Sir. I'll need someone to go with me at first, to help me find what I need. I'm reasonably sure of where everything is, but a guide wouldn't hurt the first hour or so."

"Okay, grab Bud as you leave. He can show you anything you need, or anywhere you want to go. He's been a great help to me."

The commander stood up and shook hands with John and Katy. "Again, good luck. You'll need it!"

John and Katy turned and walked out of the room. As they passed Bud, John said, "You're with me. The commander says you'll help me as long as needed."

"Fine. I'm right behind you." Bud hid a satisfied smile. His job had unexpectedly become much easier.

John kept up a fast pace, as he headed towards the bank of elevators. Katy strode along beside him, and Bud brought up the rear. As he stopped in front of the elevator door, John pushed the down button. In a few seconds the door opened, and the three of them stepped into the elevator. The door swished shut and they started to drop.

"What do you want to see first?" Bud asked John. "I can take you just about anywhere you want to go."

"I'd like to see the generators first thing. I've got a hunch that will be the place to start. I've heard that they aren't operating at full power. That could be part of the reason the shields aren't at full force."

Katy spoke up. "What about security? Are there a lot of people down here?"

"Just the operators of the machinery. No one else is allowed down here, except for a few of the guards. Fortunately, I'm one of them."

The elevator hissed to a stop, and the door swished open.

John, Katy, and Bud stepped out into the shield generator room. They stood on a platform raised about four feet off the floor.

John stepped over to the railing, and tried to take it all in. The room was huge, and five large generators stood in the middle of the floor. Large pipes and wiring ran in all directions from the generators to all parts of the room. John turned his head slowly from side to side. There was hardly any empty space in the room. Almost every inch of the walls had some kind of control or other apparatus covering it. The floor had only enough open space on it to have a few walkways.

John turned to Bud. "I'm going down to check the ejector gauges. Why don't you and Katy see if you can find me a toolbox? There should be a toolbox around with some specialized tools built especially for these machines."

With that John turned and walked down the steps to the floor.

Bud turned to Katy. "Why don't we go down to the tool room? We should find what John wants there. If not we'll keep looking till we find one."

Bud and Katy went down the stairs and turned to the right towards the tool room. Walking into the room, they started looking for a toolbox. Bud kept watching for his chance. Suddenly Katy knelt down by a bench, to check under the top. As she did so, Bud took two quick steps, crossed the threshold, and slammed the door shut. As Katy jumped up she heard the lock click shut. Bud had locked her in the tool room! And John was out on the floor by himself!

John was bending over one of the ejector gauges when Bud walked up to him. "Having any luck?" Bud asked.

"Not much yet." John replied. "All five of the ejector gauges show one hundred percent open. I'm going to have to go outside the station dome to check the ejectors themselves. I'll have to find a space suit to do that. Could you show me where they are kept?"

"Sure thing." Bud said. "I'll even help you get it on. They're on the main level. You'll have to exit through the service airlock though. They won't let you go out the front entrance."

Bud snickered. *Man. This is going to be easier than I thought. It won't be long till the station is ours.*

They walked over to the elevator, got in, and rode it up to the main floor. "I'll go over to the lockers and find you a space suit. It won't take long. If you want to go back to the service exit and wait, I'll be right along."

As John headed for the rear of the complex, Bud slipped behind an open door. Checking to be sure nobody saw him, he pulled out his radio. Thumbing the transmit switch he said, "Everything is going as planned. I'm actually ahead of schedule. Will keep you informed."

Stepping out from behind the door, Bud headed for the back of the complex. John was standing by the rear exit, waiting for him. Bud stopped by the lockers and picked out a space suit. Going on back to where John was standing, Bud said, "Here, I'll help you put it on."

John said, "Just a second. I'm going to call the base commander and let him know what I'm doing. He should know I'm going outside."

"Aw, come on John. You don't need to call the commander. I'll be right here in case you need anything. The commander would probably just tell you to go ahead, but be careful."

"Well I'm going to call him anyway. It'll just take a second." With that John put the radio up to his lips. "This is Cadet Adams, commander. I'm getting ready to go outside and check the ejectors. Just thought you might want to know"

"Okay, Cadet." The commander's voice came out of the radio. "Just be sure to take Bud with you. The station policy is to go out as a two-man team. You're not allowed to go out by yourself. Be careful."

"Okay, Bud, you heard him. Go find yourself a space suit. You're going with me."

"Now wait. You don't need me out there. I'd just be in your way. You'll be a lot better off without me. I'll just stand here by the space lock in case you need me."

"You heard the man. He said you're to go with me. Let's get moving. I've got a job to do."

Bud was becoming frantic. "Now wait. Man, I ain't never been outside the dome. I get space sick just looking out the window at the Earth. I'll just stand here and watch you."

He was visibly trembling by this time. Just then he felt a touch on his shoulder. Spinning around, he saw Katy standing there with a disrupter aimed right at him.

"Okay, you big baby. Up with your hands. John, get his gun."

As John pulled the pistol from his holster Bud croaked, "How did you get out of the tool room? I locked you in. That's supposed to be a pick proof lock."

Katy laughed. "There not a lock made that will stand up to a Ranger's disrupter. You picked a poor place to lock me up. John, you'd better get the commander out here before I show Bud just what a disrupter can do!"

John got his radio, and thumbing the transmit switch said, "Commander, could you come to the back of the complex. We've got a prisoner for you. I think you'll be surprised!"

The commander arrived promptly, and after finding out what was going on, called another guard. When he arrived, the commander said, "Take this traitor to the lockup. I want him searched thoroughly. We believe he's one of Bart's men."

The guard pulled his weapon and pointed it at Bud. "O.K., you miserable bum. Let's go!"

As the two turned to leave, Bud's radio sounded off. The voice coming from the radio said, "Glad you are ahead of schedule. Good work, Bud."

John and Katy looked at each other with astonishment, and then burst out laughing.

Chapter Seventeen

Hank was unhappy. He was going through the station personnel picture files for the third time.

"I tell you, I don't know any of these people. I don't know if Bart has any more people on the station or not. I didn't know anything about Bud until you told me you had arrested him."

"Just keep looking. If anyone at all seems even a little bit familiar, you tell me. If we're going to stop Bart, we need to know all the people he has on the station."

The security officer stood up and stretched. "I'm going to slip out and get a cup of coffee. I'll be right back." He turned and walked out the door.

As soon as he'd left, the guard walked over to Hank. "It's a good thing you haven't identified any more of Bart's people. Bart's gunning for you now. You pick out any more people, and he'll be pulling out all the stops to find you. Personally, I'd be glad if he did find you. Serve you right for working for him."

"Hey, I'm telling the truth. I don't know any more of these people. Bart's got a lot of people working for him. I can't know them all."

The officer stepped back into the room. "OK. Take him back to his cell. They're bringing Bud in for interrogation soon. I don't want the two of them in this room together."

The guard pulled his pistol, walked over to Hank, and said, "All right, let's go."

Hank got up, and the two of them left the room. When Hank got back to his cell, he walked to the back, and seated himself on the bench. Watching through the cell bars, he saw two guards escorting a man to the interrogation room.

"I knew it," Hank said aloud. "I thought that's who Bud was. He's one of the meanest men Bart has working for him. I'm sure glad he's not in here with me."

The officer questioned Bud for over two hours. After not getting much more than name, rank, and serial number from him, he turned to the guards. "Take him out of here. Put him in the same cell as the other one. Maybe if the two of them are together, they'll come up with something we need to know."

The guard escorted Bud to the holding cell. As he was shoved through the door, Hank jumped up off the bench.

"Don't put him in here with me," he screamed. "He'll murder me."

The guard snickered. "Serves you right, for pulling such a stupid stunt. You should have known better than to fire on a freighter so close to the station. Maybe he'll beat some sense into you."

Slamming, and locking the door, the guard walked away.

Chapter Eighteen

Bart was livid. "You mean to tell me they've got Bud too? How in the world did he allow himself to be caught? I don't believe this. Can't anybody over there do anything right?"

A voice came out of the speaker, "That nosy female ranger caught up with him. The last I saw, he was between two guards, heading for the interrogation room. I don't believe he's the kind to give away too much, though. I'm off duty right now, so I'll keep a watch on those two. If anything out of the ordinary happens I'll let you know."

"All right. We'll leave this frequency open for any communications."

Bart turned and strode out of the room. Going down to the deck where the ships were being outfitted, he looked for, and found, Butch. "You're with me. We're going to go to the station. I've got to find out what's going on. Things are falling apart all around us. We'll take one of the Darts. It's small enough we just might make it to the station without being noticed."

"Roger, Bart. We should make it, if we're careful. I'll go get it fired up, and ready to go. Give me ten minutes, and it should be ready."

Ten minutes later they blasted off. The small ship slithered through the asteroids like a snake through high grass.

Approaching Mars, they came in from the rear, hugging the ground to avoid the station's ancient radar. They settled down in a small cloud of red dust, about a quarter mile from the station.

Putting their helmets on, they got out of the Dart, and started trudging towards the rear of the dome. About a hundred yards from the dome, they dropped to the surface. Lying there silently, surveying their surroundings, they started crawling towards the airlock. If anybody on the station saw them before they got to it, they would be doomed. Their white space suits stood out like a spotlight against the red Mars surface.

Finally, with a last short surge, they made the airlock. Looking through the window of the lock, and seeing nobody in sight, they activated the controls. The airlock cycled and the door opened. They stepped into the lock and activated the inner door controls. The outer door shut, and with a swish of incoming air, the inner door opened. With drawn weapons, they stepped into the dome. Seeing nobody watching them, they sheathed their weapons. Turning around, Bart punched the button that shut the door. They had made it inside!

Butch pointed to the left, towards a door. Then motioning Bart to follow him, he walked over, grasped the doorknob, and tried to turn it. Locked!

"That's funny," he muttered to himself. "It's never been locked before."

Looking around, checking every direction very carefully, making sure nobody was watching him, Butch took his weapon, and placing the barrel against the lock, pressed the trigger. A bright flash, and the lock disappeared. Opening the door, he and Bart scurried inside.

Bart looked at Butch and grinned. "Well done. We're going to win this battle yet!"

Taking their suits off, they placed them on the table within easy reach in case of a hurried get away. Then going to the door, they opened it a crack, and watched the people scurrying around.

"Seems to be a busy place."

Bart laughed. "Yeah, but with any luck, enough of them won't know what they're doing, so that we can get our job done."

Butch snickered. "With any luck we'll be finished before anyone catches on. We've got enough men still out on the base to man the ships. Maybe, we ought to just go ahead and call the strike in."

Chapter Nineteen

John was just finishing checking the last ejector, when Katy tapped him on the shoulder. Turning, he looked at her through the glass of his helmet. She was standing beside him in the second space suit. She pointed towards the rear of the dome. He looked in that direction, and saw two figures peering into the airlock window. Even as he watched, the door opened, and they disappeared inside the dome. He turned, and motioned Katy to follow him. Then he headed for the door of the airlock. By the time they arrived at the door, whoever it was had disappeared.

Activating the door controls they stepped into the airlock. When it had recycled they opened the inner door. John started to step through the door when Katy grabbed his arm. As he looked at her, she shook her head no, and motioned for him to back up. Then, stepping in front of him, with a drawn ray gun, Katy crouched, and went through the door. Looking both ways, her arms swinging with her head, she saw nothing out of the ordinary. Straightening up, she motioned John to come in. He stepped through the door, and pushed the button to shut it. Once inside, they removed their helmets, and stepped out of their suits.

"I don't know who they were, or where they are," Katy said,

"But we had better inform the commander. To the best of my knowledge, there wasn't supposed to be anyone beside ourselves, outside of the dome today.

"I know. I'll get the commander on the radio." John raised the radio to his lips. "Commander, Katy and I just saw someone enter the rear dome airlock. I didn't think there was supposed to be anybody else out there."

"There wasn't. I'll be right there." Soon the commander came hurrying around the corner. "I don't suppose you had a chance to identify the two?"

"No, Sir. We were too far away. By the time we got inside, whoever it was had disappeared. It might not be important, but we thought you should know."

"It's very important, John. You two were the only ones authorized to be out. We've got a problem on our hands."

The commander pulled a radio from his pocket and spoke. "Andrews, Bolsen, report to the back airlock on the double!"

Soon two guards came rushing up. "What's the problem, Sir?" one of the guards asked.

"We've got two problems," the commander answered. "I believe we've been infiltrated. John and Katy saw two people enter this airlock while they were outside. They were supposed to be the only ones out there.

"All right, Sir. We'll commandeer some help, and do a search of the dome. If they're here, we'll find them."

"Keep me posted. I want reports at five-minute intervals. John, you and Katy, come with me."

Turning, the commander started for his office, with John and Katy following. When they arrived, he seated himself behind the desk. "What about the ejectors? Were they okay?"

Nodding his head, John answered, "Yes Sir. All five were open. No obstructions."

JOHN ADAMS - SPACE CADET

"Okay, now, about the two interlopers. Was there anything at all you can tell us that would help us identify them? What color were their space suits?"

"They were white, Sir. Just like the ones on the station. Did you notice anything different, Katy?"

"No I didn't John. I...but wait, I do remember one thing. The one in the back turned slightly, as he was entering the door. I noticed some kind of black patch on the right shoulder of his suit. I wasn't close enough to make out what it represented, but do remember it was black."

"Black! That tells me something. The pirates have a round patch on their uniforms, with skull and crossbones in the middle. That patch is black with a white center. Sounds to me like we have two of Bart's men on the station."

Picking up a microphone from the desk, the commander pressed the talk button. "Now hear this. Now hear this. All hands. We have two unidentified persons on the station. Take all necessary precautions. They are considered armed and dangerous."

John could hear the words blasting out of speakers in the center of the dome.

"Well let's hope the guards come up with whoever it is." The commander said. "Why don't you and Katy get busy on the shields? We might need them worse than ever now."

"Yes Sir! We're on our way." John and Katy turned, and exited the office.

Hurrying to the elevators, John said, "Looks like it's getting closer to the time the pirates attack. Sure hope we can get the generators going full power before that happens."

"You'll make it John. I'll help you anyway I can. We can't let the pirates get on the station. The Space Command would have to destroy the Mars Station if that happens. If the pirates do attack there will be lots of lives lost, and the station also. We'd have to start our exploration of space all over again."

"I know. That would be a tremendous setback."

Chapter Twenty

Bart and Butch had made it to a small, unoccupied office near the rear airlock. A layer of red dust covered all horizontal surfaces. A few footprints showed near the office door.

"It's a good thing you knew about this room," Bart remarked. "It's a good place to hide our suits till we get ready to leave."

"Yeah, I know." Butch replied. "This is where I'd come when I had to contact the base. Those are my footprints you see in the dust by the door."

Standing, and looking out the door, they discussed what needed to be done next.

"Let's see," Bart remarked. "They've got Hank and Bud. That leaves only Ray and Larry on the station. We've got to contact one of them and find out what's going on. Larry is a maintenance engineer on the station machinery. He might be the one to talk to. If that cadet is smart enough to figure out what he did to the shield generators we're in big trouble. Why don't you slip out, and see if you can get to the generators. Meanwhile, I'll see if I can reach him on our frequency, and alert him that you're on the way."

Opening the door a crack, Butch peered out. There was no one close enough to arouse suspicion. Butch slipped through the door, and gently closed it. Then, assuming a normal appearance, he walked slowly towards the bank of elevators. Pressing the down button, he stood there waiting while glancing around to be sure he was undetected. As the door slid open he turned to enter the elevator.

"Good morning, Lieutenant." Two guards were standing in the elevator.

Butch's heart jumped to his throat. But wait! They didn't seem to know he was wanted on the station. He stepped into the elevator.

"Good morning," he replied. "Have you heard anything about the two people that have gotten onto the station? They must have been pretty slick to manage that. Hard telling where they are by now."

He pressed the down button. The doors slid shut, and the elevator started down.

"Boy, that's for sure," one of the guards, replied. "They could be anywhere. Well, we're going to get off here, Lt. Haskell. You have a good day."

As the elevator started to slow down, the second guard suddenly perked up. *Lt. Haskell? Wasn't he the one who had escaped from the station?* he thought. *If this is him, I can't let him get away. If it's not him, I'm going to be in big trouble.*

With that the guard suddenly pulled his weapon, and placing the barrel squarely in Butch's back said, "Hold it right there. Norm, call security. If I'm not mistaken, this man is wanted. He's thought to be one of Bart's men."

"Aw, come on, Jack. Lt. Haskell has been here for a long time. He's an OK guy."

"Norm. Call security! If this guy is who I think he is, he's one of Bart's men. If not, I'll probably spend the night in the brig. Do it now!"

Stepping outside of the elevator, Norm grabbed his radio

and thumbed the talk button.

"Security, this is Anderson. We have Lt. Haskell in custody. We need confirmation that he's wanted on the station, and some help if he is."

The transmission was answered immediately.

"Hang on to him Norm. We'll be right there."

"Now look guys," Butch said. "We can work this out. Let me go, and I'll leave the base. I'll never come back to bother anyone again. Here, I'll even give you my weapon."

By this time, Norm had realized that something was amiss. As Butch reached for his weapon, Norm grabbed his arm, and pulled it away from his gun.

"Don't even think about it! Help will be here momentarily, and we'll find out what's going on."

Even as he spoke, two security personnel came rushing up. Each grabbing one of Butch's arms, and one removing Butch's gun, he said, "Good work, guys. We'll take it from here. This man is going to be put away for a long time."

As the two guards left with Butch, Norm spoke.

"I'm sure glad you were on your toes, Jack. I didn't know anything about Lt. Haskell being wanted by the command."

"Well, I just happened to remember hearing some place that he had escaped the station, and was being looked for. If it hadn't been for that, he would've probably gotten away with whatever he was planning to do. I've got a hunch it wouldn't have been pleasant."

"I think you're right. Anyway he's under control now."

"He sure won't be able to cause any trouble now. I can't say as I envy him any."

"Me either. Well, catch you later."

The two guards parted company, and walked off.

Chapter Twenty-One

Hank was standing at the front of the cell. Bud was seated at the rear. He had just finished browbeating Hank, over his identifying Butch to the interrogation officer.

Hank was half mad, half scared. He was trembling as he stood there, watching the people walk by. Suddenly, he straightened up and stared. Butch was passing by, handcuffed, between two guards. He moved over to the center of the cell door, to try and block Bud's view of the room. He was too late. He felt Bud grab him by the shoulder, and spin him around.

"Now see what you've done. Your showing Butch's picture to the authorities has caused Butch to be arrested. If they can break him were finished. Bart will kill you when he finds this out. If we weren't so exposed here, I'd do it myself. You had to go and meddle in something that you knew nothing about. Why couldn't you have kept your mouth shut, and just told them you didn't know anybody?"

"Hey, I was scared. I did that before I thought. I haven't identified anybody else. I saw Ray and Larry's pictures in the files, but never let on. As far as anybody knows, there's not anybody else on the station. If Butch will just keep his mouth shut, we should still be O.K."

"Huh. Even if we do pull this off, which is looking more

impossible all the time, you're still a dead man. Bart won't forget what you did." Bud walked to the back of the cell, and sat down. "I'm in trouble myself, but sure wouldn't want to be in the situation you're in. You're finished, boy!"

Hank turned back to the front of the cell. Staring morosely out over the crowd, he saw Larry walk by, carrying his toolbox. *Buddy,* he thought, *you'd better get out of here now, or you won't get out at all.*

As he stood there, hesitant to go back to where Bud was sitting, Ray suddenly appeared in front of him.

"Well, well. Looks like we've got two of Bart's men incarcerated. Maybe with any luck we'll get them all."

"Ray…" was the only word he got out.

He was suddenly spun violently around and shoved to the back of the cell. Bud glared at him.

"You just keep your mouth shut." Bud was furious. "Your big mouth will get him arrested too."

Turning back to Ray, he said, "You can make all the fun of us you want to. We're going to take this base away from you and use it as our headquarters. There's no way you're going to stop us."

"Yeah, yeah, I've heard people brag before. I think you're fighting a losing cause."

Glancing around to make sure no one was watching, Ray slipped Bud a note. Then, laughing, he turned and walked off.

Walking to the back of the cell, Bud opened and read the note. Then turning, he scowled at Hank.

"You just don't get it do you? If you had acted like you knew Ray, and someone had seen you, he would probably be under arrest right now. You've got to keep your big mouth shut."

"He just surprised me, walking up like that. I couldn't believe he'd come so close to the cell. It just startled me, that's all."

"Well, from now on keep your yap closed."

"I will. What's in the note anyway?"

"I shouldn't tell you but I will. The opto cannons are all installed on the ships. They just need to be charged and tested. Then we'll be ready to take over the base!"

Chapter Twenty-Two

John and Katy stepped out of the elevator door onto the raised platform above the generator room floor. He stood there looking at the machines, and thinking. Suddenly he turned to Katy. "I've got an idea. Let's go down to the main controls."

Walking up to the main control panel, he stopped and studied the power dials. "I need a toolbox. Let's see if we can find one."

They walked over to the tool room. The door was swinging back and forth on its hinges. "You did a good job on the latch, Katy. Anyone can go in and out now."

Katy laughed. "Yep. Bud should have tried something a little more difficult if he wanted to corral me. Evidently he didn't realize a Ranger could carry a disrupter on Space Command property. Of course I'm not supposed to destroy Space Command equipment, but in this case I think it was justified."

Katy walked over to the table she had looked at earlier, and knelt down to look on the shelf under the top. The steel box was still there. Inside was a set of micro adjustable tools. Just what the doctor ordered. Picking up the box, she handed it to John. They left the tool room and went back to the main control panel.

Picking an adjustable wrench, he placed it on one of the

bolts holding the cover on the panel. Pressing the trigger, the wrench sized itself to the bolt head, and then began backing the bolt out.

He looked at Katy and smiled.

"Just think how much work this would have been two hundred years ago." Placing the bolt on a table close by, he began on the second bolt. He soon had the cover off the panel.

Inside was a maze of wiring. Checking the connections on each of the five power gauges he found everything to be OK. "All right. The gauges are OK so that tells me the problem is somewhere in the generators themselves. I'm going to have to remove the covers of the turbines, and check them. Would you mind going back upstairs, and getting me the blueprints? I left them in the commander's office. You won't be gone long, and I'll be fine while you're gone."

"Sorry John. I can't leave you alone. Captain's orders."

"Go ahead. I'll be fine. You won't be gone over five minutes. I can't get in trouble in that length of time."

"Well I'm not supposed to leave you, but don't see any problem here. I'll be right back."

Katy hurried to the elevator, stepped through the door, and pushed the up button. The door slid shut.

John walked over to the first generator's turbine, and began removing the cover. He turned and placed the first bolt on a nearby table, and started to turn back, when he caught a movement out of the corner of his eye. He started to turn to see what it was, when something struck him on the back of the head. Suddenly, everything went black.

Katy knocked on the Commander's door.

"Come in."

She opened the door and stepped through. "Just came to

pick up the blueprints for John. Won't be a minute."

"How's he getting along?"

"He's just starting to remove the turbine covers. Seems to think the trouble might be in there. Well, got to go back. Can't leave him too long."

She picked up the blueprints. "Thank you. Will keep in touch." She left the office, and headed for the elevators.

She stepped out of the elevator onto the ramp, and looked over to where John was. "Got your blue…" John wasn't there! The wrench he had been using was lying on the floor.

"John. John, don't pull this on me. Come on, quit your kidding. This isn't funny."

She ran down the stairs and over to where John had been. Turning in a complete circle, she could see nothing that would give any indication of which direction John had gone. Or had been taken.

Dropping the blueprints on the floor, the disrupter appeared in her hand as if by magic. Slowly, in a slight crouch, she started walking towards the back of the generators. Looking both ways, and seeing nothing, she made a complete pass of all of the generators. Nothing! Where could he be?

As she turned to walk away from the generators, she began to silently curse herself. Why had she left him? She had disobeyed a direct order. What had she been thinking about? She was in deep trouble now.

She stopped, and surveyed her surroundings. Spying a ladder on the far wall, she walked over to it. Maybe if she climbed it a little way, she could see more of the room. She started to climb up a few rungs, then stopped and looked back over the room. Maybe if she climbed a little higher. She went up a few more rungs. Still couldn't see much better. Climbing a little higher she saw it! Hidden in the shadows, near the ceiling of the room, was a catwalk. Climbing on up to the catwalk, she walked out a few feet from the wall. Now she could see the entire room. Nothing! Examining every inch of the floor, she could see no one. Walking on out on the catwalk, she kept looking for a sign. Something, anything, to give her an idea of where John was.

She had almost walked the complete length of the room when she heard something. Standing still she listened for the sound. There! Just ahead in the shadows. A muffled sound. Standing still for a few more seconds, she began to move forward with the disrupter thrust out in front of her. She crept forward, slowly waving the disrupter from side to side as she moved.

As her eyes became more accustomed to the shadows, she saw a form on the catwalk, about ten feet ahead. She stood stock still, and watched the form. It didn't move. Suddenly, she heard the sound again. It sounded like a moan. Creeping forward, she got within about five feet of the form before she realized it was John. Running the last few steps, she kneeled down beside him. Turning him over, she saw he had been tied, hands and feet. A piece of wide tape had been placed over his mouth. Gripping a corner of the tape, she gave a quick tug, and ripped the tape off of his mouth.

"OUCH! Did you have to be so cruel? Get these ropes off of me. My head hurts."

"I'm sorry, John. If I had pulled the tape off slowly, it would have hurt a lot more." Untying the ropes she asked. "Who did this to you? Where did he go? I knew I shouldn't have left you."

John sat up, rubbing his wrists. "It wasn't your fault, Katy. I shouldn't have asked you to do what you did."

Just then Katy heard footsteps. Looking up, she saw, coming towards her, with a heavy wrench raised above his head, the figure of a man. Katy leap-froged over John, and with her head, rammed the man in the stomach. He dropped the wrench, as he bent over. It fell clattering to the floor. She spun on one leg, and, with the other, kicked the man in the head. As he staggered from the kick, she swung her fist into his chin. The uppercut did exactly what it was supposed to do. He collapsed in a heap on the catwalk.

John just sat there, his mouth agape. Shaking his head in amazement he said, "Brother! I'm glad you're not mad at me. I owe you one Katy."

"No you don't John," she said. "We're even."

Chapter Twenty-Three

Bart was beginning to become uneasy. It had been almost six hours since Butch had walked out the door. By now Bart was sure Butch had been captured. He had to get out of the station unseen. If he could hold on until dark without going nuts, he might have a chance.

He got up, and walked over to the door. Opening it a crack, he peeked out. There were too many people passing by. He silently closed the door, and walked back to the desk. Sitting down behind it, he laid his head on the desk. A little later, he would try again.

Meanwhile, Butch was still in interrogation. "You might as well come clean, Haskell. We've been at this for over five hours. All you have to do is tell us where Bart's base is. We'll do the rest. We can end this thing here and now."

"I'm not saying anything. Bart is still very dangerous. Even if you do have four of his men, he still has teeth. I wouldn't sell him too short. How is Larry doing anyway?"

"He's going to be all right. He says that banshee of a lady ranger is quick. I guess she worked him over pretty good. He still can't believe she was that fast. He's in the hospital section now, but will be in a cell soon. But let's not worry about him.

Let's worry about you. If you come clean now it'll go a lot easier on you."

"Sorry. I'm not saying anything. You'll have to find out by someone else. You might as well put me in a cell now.

"All right. Guard, get him out of here. Put him in a real cell. Let him think about this for a while.

Escorting Butch to the cell, the guard asked, "Don't you wish you had never gotten involved with Bart? Seems to me he and his operation is going to go down the drain pretty quick, now that we have that Cadet working on the generators. I guess he is one smart young man."

"Oh, I don't know. Bart is not exactly dumb. I've got a hunch he is going to fool a lot of people. I don't think I'm going to be in the cell too long. I've got a feeling everything is going to work out for him."

The guard laughed. "I don't know about that. I think you, Bart, and all his other cronies, will be in custody when this is all over. He doesn't stand a chance."

"We'll see about that."

"Yep, that we will."

Closing and locking the cell door behind Butch, the guard laughed, then spun on his heel and walked off.

Yep, Butch thought, *we'll see about that. There's going to be some very surprised people around here before this is over.*

Turning, and walking to the back of his cell, he glanced through the bars at the man in the next cell. He studied him for a second.

"Don't I know you from somewhere?"

"Yes sir, I was the pilot on the Hook."

"What happened on that ship anyway? Why did you fire on a freighter that close to the station?"

"I didn't. Hank jerked me out of the pilot's seat, sat down, and fired on the freighter himself. I begged him not to do it, but it did no good. I think he was trying to make himself look good in Bart's eyes."

"Well, it didn't work, did it? I think when we get control of the station, Hank's a dead man!"

"What's going to happen to us when they start firing on the station? Won't a lot of us be killed?"

"The pilots know where the cells are. They have orders not to fire directly at them. I just hope they're smart enough to know how to aim the cannon."

"Yeah, me too." Mike shook his head. "It does make me worry though."

Chapter Twenty-Four

"I'll be all right, really." John was speaking. "My head is sore, but it could be a lot worse. I need to get back to the generators."

"Sure," Katy said. "If you think you're up to it. You're right. It could have been a lot worse. You only took a glancing blow. If it had been a direct hit, you would be a lot sorer than you are now. We do need to get you back to the floor."

"Yeah, I'm O.K. Let's go see what we can do to help matters. If Bart does attack the station, the generators aren't going to be much help."

"You better believe, I'll keep a closer watch on you from now on. You ask me to leave you again; you'll have a bump on the other side of your head. And I'll be the one to put it there!"

John laughed. "I'll bet you could do it to."

He walked up to where he had been working on the first turbo. Picking up the wrench he finished taking the cover off. Setting it aside, he looked inside the case.

"Holy cow! Would you look at that? Someone has put the magna-rotors on backwards. No wonder they are only running half power. There's been a saboteur down here all right. Well it won't take too long to fix that. Oh, Katy, I've got some new flux filters up in my luggage. Would you go get them for me?"

Katy gave John a dirty look. "John I…"

John laughed. "I know, I know, Katy. I'm just teasing you. Let 'us' go get the filters."

Katy grinned. They headed for the elevators.

Two hours later, the magna-rotors were turned back around, and the new flux filters were installed. John walked over to the main panel and checked the gauges. They were running at full power.

"Alright. We're back up and running. There are a couple of things I want to add to the system. I think they will help even more."

Opening a side pocket of his luggage, he pulled out two circuit boards loaded with components. "This is something I picked up at the academy. They ought to add about twenty percent power to the system. If it works, we'll have about a hundred and twenty percent power out. Let Bart try and get through the shields then."

John carefully installed the boards in the first turbo case and then fastened the cover back on. He looked over at Katy. "Keep your fingers crossed," he said.

Then, picking up the radio, he pushed the transmit button. "Commander, could you come to the generator room?"

"Be right there."

Soon the commander stepped from the elevator, and walked out on the platform. "Up and running, huh?"

"Sure is, Sir. With your permission I would like to try them out."

"Permission granted."

"Fine." John walked over to the control panel. "The generators are on manual control now. After the test, if successful, I'll put them on automatic. Then if anything threatens the station, they'll start automatically."

John reached up and pressed a button. The generators whined for a second and then settled down to a steady hum. John checked each gauge one by one. Then turning to the commander he gave the thumbs up signal.

Smiling, he said, "One hundred and twenty percent power!"

"All right." The commander was elated. "Good job John. We've got the pirates beat now."

Katy raised her arms in a victory salute. "Good job, John. I knew you could do it! There wasn't any doubt in my mind."

Chapter Twenty-Five

Bart woke up, with his head on his crossed arms. *Boy, I must have dozed off,* he thought. He raised his head, and rubbed his eyes. Then, starting to get up, he stopped and stared. Standing in front of him were two guards, with smiles on their faces, and guns in their hands.

"Well, well. Lookee here what we got. It's old Bart himself. He slept right into our hands. Talk about easy."

Bart started to get up.

"Easy Bart. Sit back down and keep your hands on the table. We'll tell you when to get up. The commander has been notified, and will be here any minute. He'll tell us what to do with you."

The commander walked into the room. "Good work, men. Let's take him to a cell. We'll decide what to do with him later."

Motioning him to get up, the guards, one on each side of him, marched him outside the room.

As they were taking him to his cell, he asked, "Couldn't the three of us work something out? I bet we could reach some kind of agreement before my men get here. When they get here there won't be much left of this place. The three of us could fit in my ship, and escape this place before they get here."

"I don't think so," one of the guards said. "It's my understanding the shields are fixed. I guess the young cadet is quite a whiz around machinery. They say he has even got the generators running at more than a hundred percent. We'll be perfectly safe here. In fact, we'll be safer here, than your men in their ships. When the cadet got more than one hundred percent power out of the shields, he increased the stiffness of the surface. Now, instead of the shields absorbing the light of the opto cannons, they will reflect the light. Opto cannons, as good as they are, have one bad habit. They reflect. If they reflect off our shields, the reflections are liable to cut up their own ships. Could be quite a massacre out there."

Bart turned white as a sheet. "You mean my own men could be killed?

"That's right. If the reflections bounce back onto a ship, it'll cut just as bad as if the cannon had aimed at the ship. Just because the light bounces, doesn't mean it won't cut. It will."

"Oh my God! Get me a radio. I've got to call the base. Jan has got to tell the men to call the whole thing off. I can't have this on my conscience."

Chapter Twenty-Six

The Station Commander had called a special meeting of all station personnel. After a short speech of congratulations to all, for a job well done, he asked, "Will Space Cadet John Adams please come forward?"

John stepped up to the commander.

"Cadet Adams, for meritorious duty to the Mars Station, I am proud to award you the Mars Station Medal of Honor." With that the commander pinned the medal to John's uniform, then stepped back and saluted him. John returned the salute.

"Thank you, Sir."

A few minutes later, they were seated around a large table, celebrating their victory.

"Just think," the commander was saying. "Because of John and Katy, the Mars Station is unharmed, the pirate base has been destroyed, and Bart and his men are all in custody. And not a shot has been fired. It was smart of Bart to give us the location of his base. If he hadn't, and his men had attacked the station, there could've been lots of casualties."

"Yes, it's worked out pretty good. There was a time or two when I began to wonder if everything was going to be all right."

John thought for a moment. "You know, Bart was plenty smart at that. He had a man in the academy, a man on the moon base, and a man on that Space Command ship. Not to mention the men on the station. He knew how to infiltrate."

"Yes he did." the commander said. "He was no dummy, I'll give you that. By the way, John, how did you get that bump on your head?"

Oh Oh, Katy thought. *Here it comes. I'm in trouble now.*

"Oh that," John said. "I get clumsy once in a while. I was working on the turbo, when I slipped backwards, and hit my head on the generator. I did wipe the blood off, though, Commander."

John, I could kiss you, Katy thought. *Thanks for saving my life!*

The commander laughed. "I don't think a little blood would keep the generator from working. By the way, do you know what you are going to do next?"

"My orders are supposed to arrive in a few days. I won't know until they get here."

"Well, you two enjoy your stay. I've got to get back to the office. Still got paperwork to do. These last few days have doubled my work load." The commander got up and left the table.

"Well John," Katy said. "I've sure enjoyed working with you. I'm leaving for Earth in less than an hour. Hopefully I'll be able to see you again one of these days soon. And thanks for that little white lie. You saved me a lot of trouble."

"No problem, Katy. And I'm sure we'll meet up again. Our careers aren't over yet. And I hope the next time I'm required to have a backup, it'll be someone as good as you. If you hadn't been here, I wouldn't have gotten the job done."

"Thanks for the kind words, John. But since I've come to know you, I figure you would have made it with or without me."

"Don't bet on that, Katy. If it hadn't been for you, I would never have made it off the moon shuttle."

"Well, maybe I did help just a little bit. But you did your part too. Well, take care. Maybe we'll see each other again one of these days."

With a wave of her hand, Katy turned and walked away.

As John sat there watching her leave, he thought aloud, "Wonder if I'll ever see her again?"

* * * * *